Max
and the
Tag-Along
Moon

For Dayton and Kai—
always remember the view from the backseat!

PUFFIN BOOKS
Published by the Penguin Group
Penguin Group (USA) LLC
375 Hudson Street
New York, New York 10014

USA * Canada * UK * Ireland * Australia
New Zealand * India * South Africa * China

penguin.com
A Penguin Random House Company

First published in the United States of America by Philomel Books,
a division of Penguin Young Readers Group, 2013
Published by Puffin Books, an imprint of Penguin Young Readers Group, 2015

THE LIBRARY OF CONGRESS HAS CATALOGED THE PHILOMEL BOOKS EDITION AS FOLLOWS:
Cooper, Floyd.
Max and the tag-along moon / Floyd Cooper.
p. cm.
Summary: When Max leaves his grandfather's house, the moon follows
him all the way home, just as Grandpa promised it would.
978-0-399-23342-5 (hardcover)
[1. Moon—Fiction 2. Grandfathers—Fiction.] I. Title.
PZ7.C78485Max 2012
[E]—dc23
2011049784

Puffin Books ISBN 978-0-14-751546-9

Edited by Tamra Tuller

Paintings were created using a subtractive process. The medium is mixed media.

Printed in the United States of America

9 10 8

Max and the Tag-Along Moon

and the Moon

PUFFIN BOOKS
An Imprint of Penguin Group (USA)

Floyd Cooper

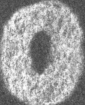ne night, as Max was leaving Granpa's
house, he reached up to give Granpa a big
hug good-bye. In the sky behind Granpa appeared
a big fine moon.

"Look, Granpa, the moon!"

"That ol' moon will always shine for you . . .
on and on!"

Granpa and Max gazed quietly at the big moon
together as it embraced them in soft yellow light.

Max smiled at the moon and Granpa, then climbed into the car.

"Bye-bye, Granpa! Bye-bye, moon!"

As the car pulled away, Max kept his eyes on Granpa until he disappeared from sight, and all he saw was the moon.

Max kept his eyes on that moon, waiting for it to disappear, too.

The long ride home was
swervy-curvy. This way
and that, all the way.
And the moon seemed
to tag along.

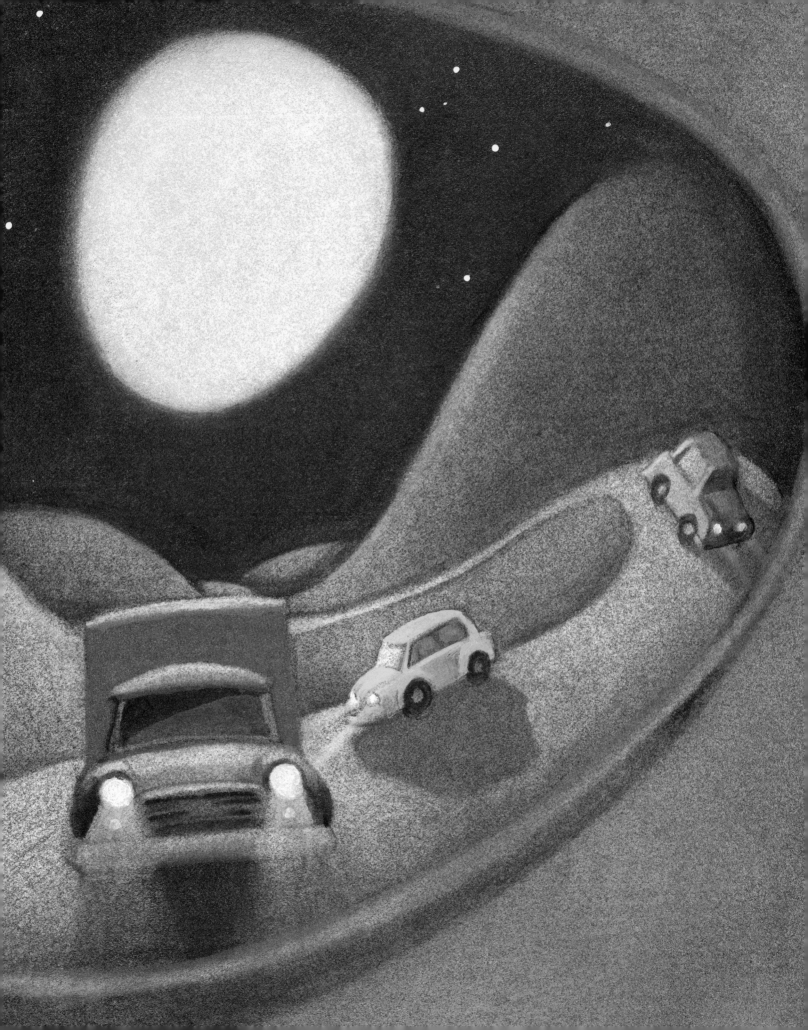

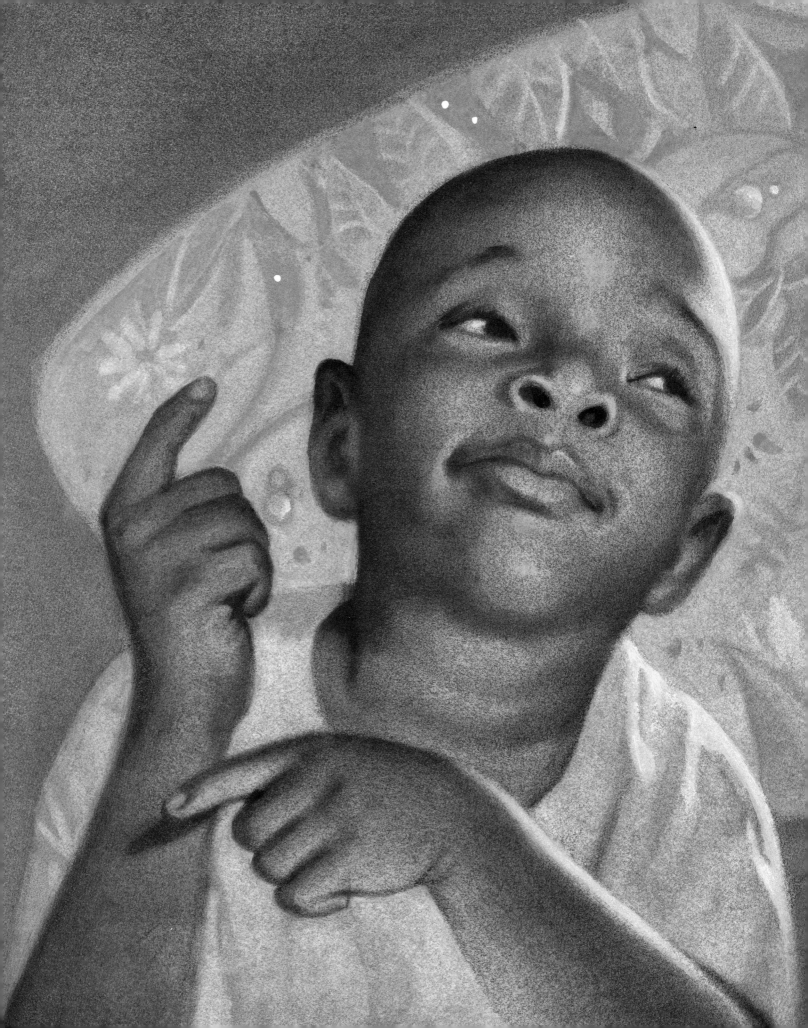

Max giggled as he watched the beautiful bright orb flicker through the passing trees, trailing behind the car as it traveled home, this way and that, playing peekaboo.

Up a hill, down a hill, the moon
was ever there. Over a bridge, around
a curve, the moon bounced along!

Around a tree, past a field of
sleeping cows, the moon stayed
quietly with Max.

Through a small town with
roundabout streets, Max gazed
as the moon kept up.

At the mouth of a tunnel and out the other end, Max smiled when he saw the moon there, waiting.

Dark clouds tumbled across
the night sky. The stars and
nightingales all faded away.

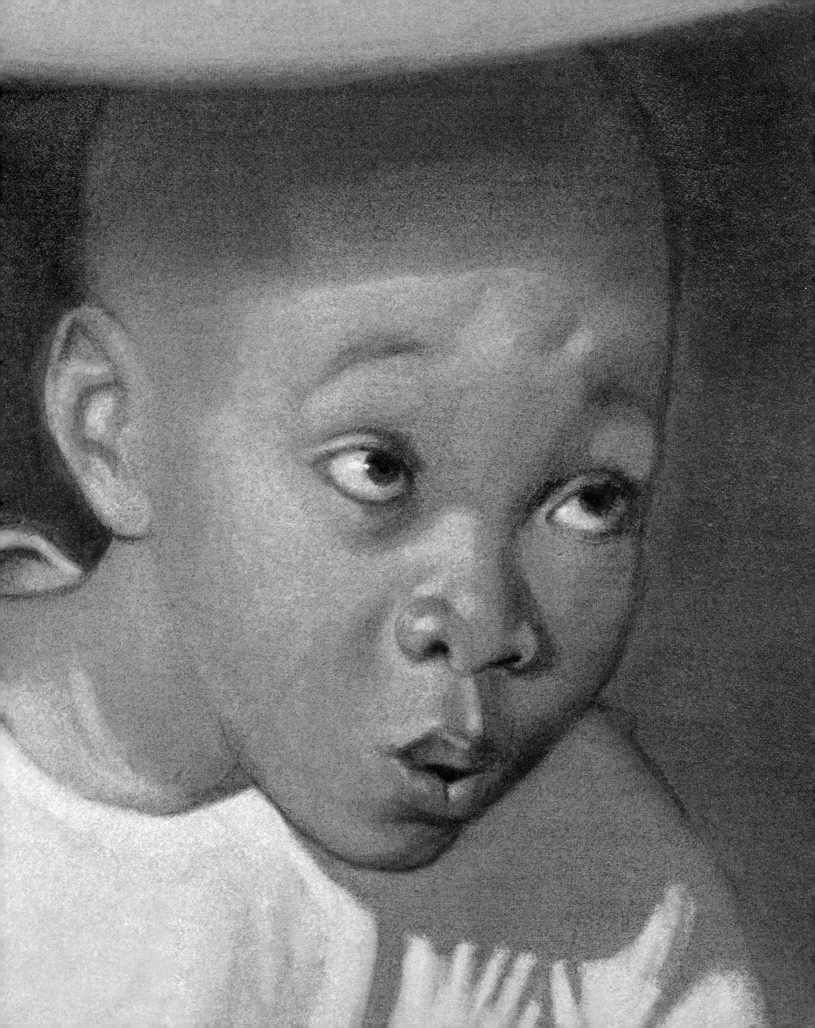

Max searched the darkness and
wondered, where is the moon?
Granpa said it would always shine
for me.

Finally home, Max took one last look
up at the empty night sky.
    "I guess that ol' moon couldn't shine
for me all the way home."

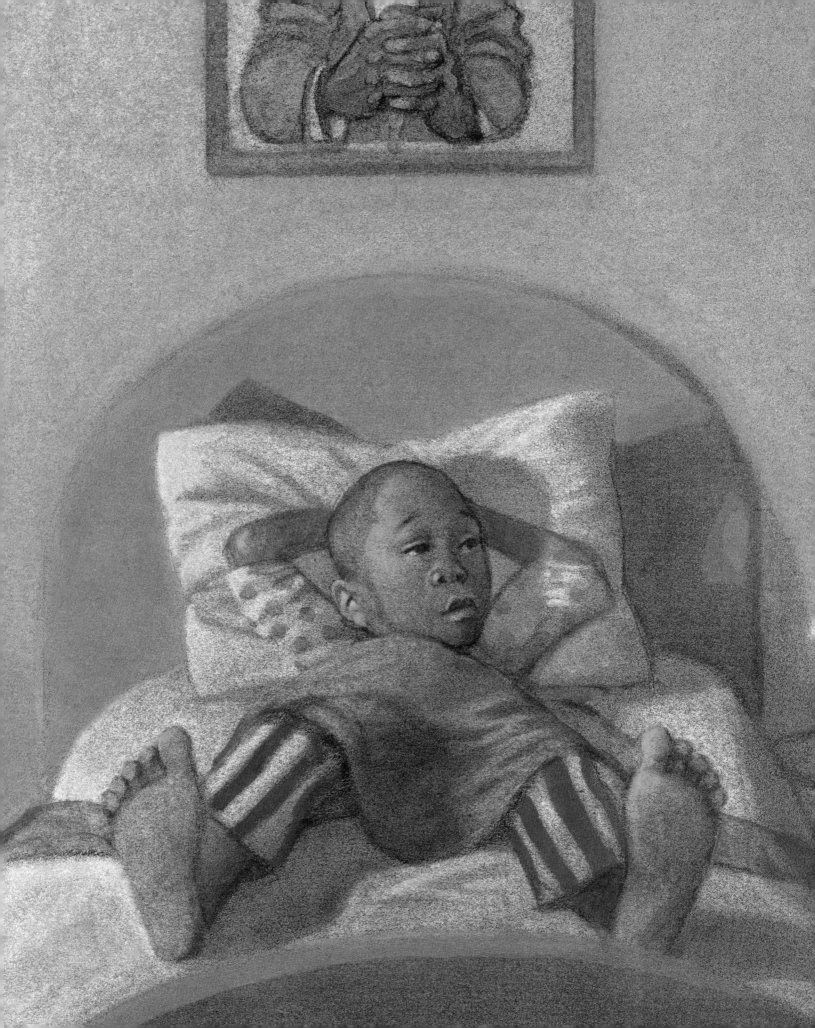

Upstairs in bed, the room
was dark. Max felt alone. He
missed Granpa. He missed that
tag-along moon.

Then slowly, very slowly, Max's
bedroom began to fill with a soft yellow
glow. The clouds faded away and the
moon peeked through!

Max gazed up at that magic ball of light
and thought about what Granpa said.
"That ol' moon will always shine
for me . . . on and on!"

Max knew then that whenever he saw the moon,
he would think of Granpa, on and on.
And he slept soundly, embraced in soft yellow light.